Erotic Sex Stories

An Erotica Collection of Explicit Adult Encounters, Full of Orgasmic Threesomes, Rough Anal, First Time Lesbian, Hardcore Gangbangs, Spanking, Domination, Role-Play, and More!

Mia Foster

Contents

Story 1: A Guest for A Night

♥

"Welcome to my apartment. It's not much, but it's home."

Anna glanced around. She ran her fingers through the wall as she walked in. Corbin followed from behind, wringing his hands. He hoped she wouldn't be disappointed.

It was a modest apartment, with a well-furnished living room, kitchen, bedroom, and bathroom. That was about it.

She looked back at him, beckoning him over with a finger.

"So, um, do you need anything? To eat, drink, or...?"

"We're coming from a bar. Also, I already had dinner. Thanks for the offer."

Corbin clenched his fingers. Ouch.

"Alright, then. Is there –"

"Why did you bring me here?" she asked, cutting him short.

Corbin didn't skip a beat. "I find you attractive. Very attractive. But don't worry. I don't have any ill intentions. Just wanted to...to help."

"I'm not worried about that." She glanced around. "Can I use your bathroom?"

His lips pursed before he answered. "Sure thing. Last door down the hallway."

Anna flashed him a smile that made his chest flutter, before striding into the hallway. As her figure disappeared from view, he sighed.

Corbin sunk into a couch nearby. Anna's mysteriousness intrigued him. She'd caught his eye earlier that evening at the Dead Rabbit, a popular cocktail lounge he frequented. Here was this mysterious but beautiful woman sitting across him, sipping her wine. He could tell she wasn't from around here. Her English had an accent but he couldn't tell what it was. He was right. She was Georgian. Somehow, he convinced her to stay the night at his apartment.

"Aren't you coming to sleep? It's pretty late."

Corbin jumped, then turned. She was wearing a towel, and her long, black hair – which was still damp – was swept over her shoulders. He swallowed. Her silvery-grey eyes stared into his blue ones.

He grinned, running his hand through his hair. "I was thinking of sleeping here."

"In the living room? No. Isn't your bed big enough for the two of us?" She raised an eyebrow.

"It is."

She stretched out a hand. "Then let's go."

Soon they were in his room. Moonlight illuminated the bedroom through the open windows. Corbin found it hard to meet Anna's eyes, so he found himself looking away often. His towel was still on her.

"Um, I have a t-shirt you can wear for the night if you want. Also, you can have the blanket."

He rubbed his sweaty palms together. He'd been with women before. He was never nervous around them. With this woman, it was different. She had an aura about her that attracted him, but he was being cautious.

"Do we need clothes?"

Corbin turned to Anna and his breath lodged in his throat. Her towel was off, revealing a body he could only describe as *divine*. Her creamy, curvy tits weren't big or small. They were perfect – just the right size. Her slender waist was inviting, giving way to ample thighs and long, smooth legs.

There was no way he could resist. Within moments, she was in his arms. Their lips met, brushing across each other. His tongue dipped between the seam of her lips. Their tongues stroked as they met.

To Corbin, foreplay was unnecessary on a normal day. Sex was usually straightforward – a kiss, quick make-out and soon he was buried deep in an eager cunt. With Ana, it was different. He could kiss her for hours.

Time passed. Neither of them knew how many minutes they spent exploring the crevices of each other's mouths. Corbin had only one thing on his mind – he had to feel her. He moved his hand to her breast, smoothing his palm across her nipple.

Anna was already turned on, with liquid heat between her thighs. Corbin's erection pressed against her thighs through the fabric of his jeans. He didn't attempt to hide it. It was long and thick, straining the denim. He was hung, that was for sure. It was something he was proud of.

She reached out, stroking his erection as their mouths met each other. Corbin broke the kiss as he moved his tongue to the base of her chin. She arched her neck, inviting him. He took the offer and moved his tongue along her pale skin.

Her fingers worked on unbuttoning his shirt, and soon he wriggled out of the sleeves. The shirt fell to the carpet. Her hands moved to the fastenings of his trousers. She attacked his belt and the zipping with urgency.

He groped her full breasts and pinched her nipples. A slight moan escaped her throat as his fingers brushed across them.

Anna pulled down his pants and underwear as soon as she undid the fastenings, revealing his larger-than-normal-sized cock. She licked her lips.

"You have an impressive cock. Can I have a taste?" The words came out as a whisper.

Corbin grinned. "Be my guest."

As she went to her knees and got down to business, he ran his fingers across her hair. He exhaled sharply as she began sucking. She worked the head at first. He groaned as she moved her mouth down his length with much skill.

Corbin ran his fingers through his hair, throwing his head back. Here was this mysterious woman going to town on his cock. He had never had it this good.

She kept on sucking on his cock. She reached down and rubbed her dripping wet clit as she grew more aroused.

"Damn!" Corbin said in admiration as she continued. "You know what you're doing, don't you?"

She nodded as she took his cock deep into her throat. Corbin's eyes rolled back as he pulled her head even closer. No woman had taken him this deep before. She drew him out of her mouth and teased the crown of his cock with her slippery satin tongue.

Corbin closed his eyes and guided her head closer. He plunged his cock deep into the base of her throat and released his seed with a loud grunt.

"Fuck. That was intense."

He drew his cock out of Anna's mouth. He sat on the bed, heaving deep breaths. She stood and strode over to him, stopping inches from his face.

"Care to return the favor?" she asked.

He chuckled. "For sure."

"Lie back."

Corbin did as she asked. She climbed onto the bed and moved over to him. Angling herself, she sat on his face. Her pussy was directed atop his mouth. She shivered as he moved his tongue. Grabbing his hair, she gyrated around his face. She threw her head back, taking one hand to her right breast.

Corbin wasn't new to this. As his tongue moved around the opening of Anna's cunt, he pinched her clit with his fingers. A flood of pleasure washed over her, overwhelming her senses. Her cries of ecstasy grew louder and she writhed against his face. He lapped at the juices, which flowed freely from her cunt, savoring the taste.

Anna lifted her cunt off Corbin and fell on the bed. He sat up, gazing at her figure. Her breasts heaved up and down as she took deep breaths. He grinned as a thought came to him.

"Wanna take a quick shower?

She nodded, and Corbin helped her up. Holding her hand, he led her to the bathroom.

Inside, Corbin turned on the shower and a cascade of warm water washed down their bodies. Soon the glass walls were clouded by steam. He came in behind her, kissing her neck. She swept her hair over her shoulder to offer his tongue better access. He fondled her breasts, brushing over her nipples. One hand traveled lower to the opening of her cunt. He stroked her clit with two fingers and she wriggled against his erect cock.

"I want you inside me," she said, moaning.

He didn't need any more prompts.

She leaned against the glass, bending over to present her pussy to him. He pushed the top of his cock inside her. He moved his hips, going deeper with every thrust. Then he plowed his full length in with a swing of his hips. She was dripping wet and ready for him. Loud raspy moans escaped her mouth.

She moved her hips to meet his, taking him even deeper. Corbin was having a hard time keeping up with her as she ground her hips against him. He held her waist to control the pace and pinned her against the glass with his strokes.

Her moans – incessant at this point – echoed through the walls of the bathroom. He grabbed her hair and moved his hips even faster. Moments later, she screamed as a writhing orgasm overtook her.

Corbin had had enough at this point. He had to come. He just wasn't going to be able to hold it any longer. Never before had he had sex as intense as this. This mysterious woman whom he met just hours ago gave him a pleasure he never imagined possible. He moved with an intensity that consumed a lot of his energy. It was overwhelming, even for him. He clenched his teeth. He was on the edge.

"Fuck, I'm .... I'm close. I'm close, Anna!" His voice was rough and primal.

"Come ... do it in me," she said in between moans.

"Is ... is it safe?"

"It ... it is. Come in me. I want to feel you. I want ... to feel you inside me."

Corbin hunkered down and pressed deeper into her. Closing his eyes, he drove his cock deep into her one final time. Shuddering, she leaned into his arms. He pressed against her as uncontrollable waves of pleasure washed over him. He pulled his cock out after a while and some drops of his cum landed on the wet bathroom floor.

"That was intense."

She leaned into his arms. "Yes, it was."

"Should we go back to bed? My legs feel like jelly."

"I'd like that."

The night wasn't over yet for Corbin and Anna. Not by a long shot.

Story 2: A First-timer's Fantasy

♥

"Diego? You here?"

Brian opened the door to Diego's room an inch and glanced around. There was no sign of his best friend. Sighing, he closed the door. Where could Diego have gone?

Diego had told him earlier that afternoon he was going to lunch with Jane, the new transfer student. That was four hours ago. Brian bit his lips. God, Diego was so lucky. Jane was hot and everyone knew it. Her long, blonde hair was always in a ponytail. Her oval face was complete with stunning features – striking green eyes, a straight nose, and full lips. Her petite, chubby figure was complete with curves that always had men staring. Brian included.

How did Diego get a lunch date with her? She was very reserved, so it was hard for anyone to ask her out.

A call came into Brian's phone. It was Diego.

"Dude! Where did you go? Been looking all over the place for you!"

"Forget that. Are you in the dorm?"

"Uh, yeah! I just checked you up on your room but–"

"I need you here, ASAP. I'm here with Jane in our department. We're at the class Professor Fudge uses for World History."

The call ended, leaving Brian scratching his head. Why was he needed? A study session? He was a geek, after all.

Brian hurried over to the department building. He took extra care, slipping past the janitor and the night guard who were talking about baseball. He was soon at the lecture room Diego specified. A fluorescent lightbulb was on. He went in and found Diego making out with Jane, seated on a bench.

Brian's jaw dropped. "What ... the fuck?"

Diego and Jane broke off their kiss. Diego waved at Brian.

"Come on, Brian! Come join us!"

Join them? This must be a joke. Were they trying to prank him?

Jane went over to a dumbstruck Brian and planted a quick kiss on his lips. His eyes widened in surprise.

Okay. This was not a prank.

"Wha... what's going on?"

"I've wanted to fuck the both of you for a while now. I have a thing for nerds and cool guys, especially if they're best friends."

Brian adjusted his glasses. He swallowed. Diego came in behind Jane and fondled her breasts through the thin fabric of her blouse.

True, Brian was a nerd. Heck, he was still a virgin at twenty-one! Diego on the other hand was one of the college's cool guys. Jane wanted to be fucked by a nerd and a cool guy at the same time? An interesting fantasy.

As if drawn by an invisible force, Brian's hands moved to the buttons on Jane's blouse. She wore nothing underneath. There was a pause, as if Diego and Brian were waiting for approval from Jane.

Jane's breasts were beautiful. The prospect of fondling those fresh and succulent tits caused Brian to shiver in anticipation.

"What are you waiting for?" she said to Brian.

Diego grinned. "Go ahead, man. Feel those awesome tits."

His trembling fingers traveled to her breasts. He gulped. He pressed them, slowly at first, then with increased vigor as his confidence grew.

Diego kissed Jane from behind. She drew his head closer as their tongues met. He moved his hands to her skirt, drawing it down. Breaking off the kiss, Jane took her fingers to Brian's pants and unzipped them. He stepped out of them as they fell to the floor. She dragged down his boxers and gasped when she saw his cock. Brian was huge. Her face was flustered, but she couldn't take her eyes off Brian's erection.

"Touch his cock," Diego said in a husky voice.

Brian's heart raced with anticipation. He planted his legs apart and she knelt on the ground between them. She wet her hands with her spit and wrapped them loosely around his length. She started moving them up and down.

"Wow. That feels so good." Brian said, throwing his head back.

Jane stood. Brian raised his eyebrows, wondering why she stopped. She wiggled her hips for both guys, then pulled her panties down in one fluid motion. She was completely naked.

Diego whistled. "Fuck, Jane, you look so fucking sexy."

Brian's cock got harder.

Diego pointed to a desk nearby. "Lie on this desk, face up. Make sure your hips are on the edge. We're gonna give you the time of your life."

Without hesitation, Jane did as she was told. She spread her legs wide.

"Alright, boys. Who's getting a taste of this meal?" she asked.

"That would be you, Brian. I'm getting this cock in her mouth."

Brian's heart raced. He swallowed. He would never have thought he'd be down there, eating Jane's pussy, not in his wildest dreams. After a moment's hesitation, he knelt. His hands went to her knees, placing them on his shoulders as he kissed her thighs. She squirmed a little.

His kisses went higher until he parted her pussy with his lips, and started licking her entrance. Her body was rocked by the sensation, and she arched her back. Brian kept her in place with his hands on her hips as he sucked, kissed, and licked her dripping cunt.

Diego stepped forward and let his pants and underwear fall to his knees. Angling his erect cock close to Jane's face, he waited for a moment. As she parted her lips in a moan, he thrust into her mouth. His hand curled in her hair, holding her face still. He pulled back for a moment before thrusting into her mouth again.

Brian pressed her clit with his lips and she moaned, writhing under his hands. Diego pressed his cock further into her mouth. Her small cries of pleasure encouraged Brian. He watched her suck Diego's cock with vigor, and the sight nearly brought him to climax. She drew her head in closer, sliding her tongue against the side of his cock. He groaned as his cock reached the base of her throat.

Diego increased his speed until he was thrusting into her mouth at a rapid pace. She gagged, coughing. Brian was still lapping at her cunt, but he was now pressing a finger into her entrance. She shuddered, pulling his head closer. Without warning, he stopped and stood.

Stepping closer, he rubbed his erection over her clit. He circled his cock, teasing her. She gasped, trembling at the sensation. Then, he slid his cock down to her entrance and stayed put. Her breathing became harsher, and she gripped either side of the small desk.

"Fuck that cunt!"

Diego's encouragement spurred Brian on.

Brian drew in a deep breath. It was his first time. He shivered. His heart was drumming and he took deep breaths.

Her pussy stretched, letting in his large size and squeezing tightly around his girth. He filled her up with his slow thrust, trying to find a rhythm. He thrust into her again, and she took every inch he had to offer. Her moans were muffled by Diego's cock which was still in her mouth.

Brian pulled back a little before pressing in again. She brought her legs up to hug his hips, urging him deeper. Holding her waist, he plunged into her. His hands grew tighter on her hips and his pace began to build. It was exhilarating, The desk creaked with every thrust.

"Damn, what a scene we have here." Diego whistled.

It was a scene indeed. Jane was on the desk, sucking on Diego's cock while Brian rammed her pussy. This was better than his wildest erotic dreams.

Jane's body trembled as a tremor shook her to the core.

Diego's loud groan filled the room. Jane kept working his cock like it was a lollipop. He slipped past her lips, driving further into her mouth. Grunting, he pulled out. He stroked his cock and soon he was releasing cum over her mouth and breasts.

Brian was still going. He could tell he was close. She arched her back a little. She let out a long moan, before rotating her hips. Behind her, Diego sat on the desk to watch.

"Come for me, Brian! Fucking come on my tits," she said.

Brian grunted, leaning forward so that his head was against her chest for the last few thrusts. He pulled out, letting his semen spill out of his cock onto her tummy and her breasts. Brian collapsed into a chair nearby, panting. Diego got a towel out of his bag and helped wipe her body. Her tits still glistened with cum from both men.

Diego laughed. "What a way to spend the night. Right, Brian?"

"Yeah. It was awesome. Uh, are you alright, Jane?" Brian asked as Jane remained at the table.

Jane gave a thumbs up. Her chest heaved as she took deep breaths. Crazy night.

Brian kept his gaze on her. "You're ... um, beautiful, you know."

Jane sat up, extending her arms. "Come here, you sweet boy."

She wrapped her arms around his waist and kissed him as he got closer. Diego came in from behind, pressing his cock against her back.

"Both of you ready for another round?" Diego said.

"Let Brian catch his breath first. She winked at him. "Must have been a wild ride for a first time."

14

Story 3: Spanking the Secretary

♥

"Hello, sir. You asked me to wait behind earlier?"

Alex Van Hagel rested his chin on his knuckles as his secretary, Dorothy, stood by the doors of his office. He'd had enough of her teasing him with her well-rounded butt. Anytime she came into his office, she always found an excuse to bend over. He had a rule: business and pleasure were two worlds apart. Dorothy was a threat to that rule.

She had asked for it. Now, she was going to get it.

Dorothy smiled. She knew what she was doing. She wanted her boss to spank her. Her greatest turn-on had always been a slap on the ass. Alex was a playboy – a very handsome one, and she knew it. His features included his long, golden hair and a pair of striking blue eyes. His thick, toned hands on her butt cheeks were all she could think of any time she was around him. So what if she had to act clumsy around him so she could always tease him? At a point, he wouldn't be able to help himself.

Her smile morphed into a grin. She was counting on it.

"Hello, Dorothy. I asked you to stay behind for an important reason."

"What's that, Mr. Hagel?"

He lay back on his swiveling chair, staring into her eyes. He cleared his throat.

"Your ass."

Dorothy raised an eyebrow. "I'm sorry, Mr. Hagel?"

He leaned forward. "Your fucking ass. It's had me going nuts. You've been pushing your ass at my face with every fucking chance you get, and you have to pay for that."

"I don't … I'm afraid I don't…understand you, Mr. Hagel. My ass?"

Her voice was shaky. She hadn't expected an approach so brazen.

Alex got up and walked across the room to Dorothy. She took a step back as he came within inches of her. His hand went to her face, rubbing her chin. His fingers moved to her lips. She clasped her lips shut, unsure of herself. After a while, her lips parted and two fingers slipped inside. She sucked on the fingers as heat gathered in her core.

"See? You're a slut, Dorothy, and you need to be punished like one." He pointed to his oak desk. "Lean against it. Stick out your big ass to me."

Hesitating, she walked toward his desk. He slapped her butt and the contact sent tingles of excitement running down her spine. She bent over, offering a tantalizing glimpse of her curves.

Alex grinned. "Now, do you know what I'll do to you?"

Dorothy swallowed. Whatever was on her boss's mind, it had something to do with her ass. It always did whenever she was with a man.

She shook her head. "No, Mr. Hagel. Tell me."

"I'm going to hit you. Then, you'll grind your ass on my cock. I won't stop spanking you. Finally, I'll fuck you as you are while spanking you. Your ass is going home tonight all red."

The thrill of wanting to be spanked washed over Dorothy. She wiggled her butt to her boss, who licked his lips at sight. He groped her ass cheeks, before slapping both. A soft moan left her lips. He drew her skirt up to her hips.

He rubbed his chin. "Nice panties."

"I'm glad you like it, sir."

Grinning, Alex spanked her once more. Her gorgeous, pale bottom was already reflecting his handprints. He spanked a little harder, over and over again until he had hit her almost a dozen times. Dorothy's adorable ass wriggled as he rested his hand on the reddened cheeks.

He slid his hands up her thighs and between her cunt. He stuck his middle finger inside her and she squirmed. He stuck another finger in her pussy, fucking her with his two fingers for a moment. She was so wet her pussy juices dripped down her thighs and all over his two fingers down to the last knuckles.

"Why are you so fucking wet?"

Her voice was shaky. "I...I don't know, sir. I think I'm wet because you spanked me."

"I'm going to punish you for this. Get on your knees."

Dorothy knelt in her heels, facing Alex's bulge in his pants.

"Take off my belt."

She tried to take off his belt with trembling hands but fumbled. All her poise had vanished minutes ago in a haze of horniness. It took repeated attempts for her to slide it off.

"Hurry up. I don't have all day."

She took out his cock from underneath his pants and bought her head closer. She kissed the tip.

"You're going to suck my cock now. You're going to show me how much you want me, and how grateful you are that I taught you a lesson."

Sucking in a quick breath, she stroked his cock. She marveled at how thick her boss's cock was. She could barely get her fingers around his girth. She took him into her mouth, lapping at his cock with her tongue. She tried to take him deep down her throat but gagged on the first attempt.

He grinned. "Can't handle my cock?"

Dorothy shook her head. Her tongue traced a line to his balls. Then she moved back to his stiff hard cock. As her mouth moved to the head, he shoved the full length down her throat, hitting the base. She was close to gagging, but she forced air into her nose and relaxed her throat to take him in even deeper. He groaned, fucking her mouth until tears streamed down her face.

Dorothy took Alex's cock deep in her throat again. Then he pulled out.

"That's enough. Turn around."

She turned, swallowing and closing her eyes shut. It would be coming anytime now.

Smack!

He spanked her so hard she squealed. It was followed by five more in a row. He plunged his fingers into her again – three, this time. He was stretching her. Soon she was squirting all over his fingers and hand. Her moans reverberated around the office.

"Stand up. Take off your clothes.

" It wasn't a request.

Dorothy stood up, unbuttoning her blouse. It fell to the floor, along with her bra. Her ample tits bounced as the bra slid off. She pulled her skirt and panties down, before stepping out of them.

"Damn, Dorothy.You look so fucking gorgeous."

She blushed. Turning, she wiggled her naked, reddened ass at Alex. He undressed in a hurry, tossing all his clothes away. He came closer and slapped her ass cheeks again.

"Bend over."

She leaned on his desk and he came in behind. He held her waist, leaning in.

"You're a dirty girl, and I'll treat you like one."

"Yes, Mr. Hagel. Punish this dirty girl."

Dorothy's chest fluttered. She couldn't wait to be fucked hard from behind by Alex's big, erect cock. Plunging into her wet pussy, he rubbed her clit with the same rhythm. The motion of his hard fingers on her made her quiver. He stopped just before she climaxed.

"You're not allowed to come."

Alex's voice was thick and raspy. He spanked her butt again as he pulled out.

"We're not done yet. Get on all fours." His voice carried a tone of command.

Dorothy went on her hands and knees. She arched her back and stuck her ass out. Alex slid his fingers inside her pussy. He tapped an ass cheek with his free hand.

"I'm going to make you squirm," he said in a raspy tone.

Alex spat on two of his fingers. He bore both fingers into her asshole, pushing in and out. He drove his cock back into her pussy and thrust with rapid speed. She was being stretched in both holes.

Alex was fucking his secretary with his two fingers still in her asshole, pumping in and out. Sweat dripped from his brows but he didn't attempt to wipe it off. He spanked her cheeks with his other hand and Dorothy collapsed onto the carpet. After a few minutes, Alex's breathing became labored and his grip tightened around Dorothy's thighs. She shuddered, shaken by the intensity of her orgasm. He spanked her again. Soon, her gasps and screams echoed around the office.

Dorothy's cunt convulsed as she squirted onto the floor, her legs, and Alex's thighs. He groaned as he pulled himself out of her. The cool air in the room blew against her wet, heated pussy and ass.

He slapped her ass, before rubbing his hands on his cock. He pumped himself fast until he came all over her butt cheeks and back. Then he took a step back, taking deep breaths.

"Fuck. That took a lot out of me," he said, drawing a ragged breath.

Dorothy giggled. "At least you punished me well, Mr. Hagel."

Alex extended a hand to Dorothy, who promptly took it. As she got up, he caressed her ass, which was coated with his cum.

"I still can't get enough of this."

Alex was hard again. A corner of Dorothy's lips curved up.

"Care to punish this bad girl once more?" She wiggled her butt at him.

He grinned. "With pleasure."

Story 4: Submission to Pleasure

♥

"You have a beautiful house, Zack. Neat. I like it."

Zack chucked as Bridgette surveyed his house. It was true the design of his duplex was fascinating, but he didn't bring her here to compliment it.

Just an hour ago, they were at a dinner party hosted by his friend, a business tycoon named Robson. Zack was meeting Bridgette for the first time that night, but the French-American model intrigued him. They hit it off immediately as they had engaging conversations on certain matters. When Zack invited her to his home, she accepted without hesitation.

"Thanks. I'm a man of good taste."

She turned to face him. "At the party, when we were talking about the best genres of fiction, you mentioned something interesting."

"Any erotica treating domination and submission. I still go by it."

"Why does that form of erotica appeal to you?"

Zack grinned. "Simple. I like being in control. When you control everything, it's more fulfilling."

Bridgette ran her fingers along the mantelpiece of his fireplace. Interesting.

"Does this mean that you're a Dom?" She kept her gaze on the fireplace.

He stepped closer to her. "I am. Or at least I try to be."

Her face flushed. "Care to... to show me your methods?"

"Are you asking me to fuck you as a Dom would?"

She smiled. "You could say that."

"Can you handle it? I'm asking for good measure."

She brought her face closer to his. Her warm breath caressed his cheekbones.

"Try me." It came out as a whisper.

"Alright, then. Follow me."

He held her hand, leading her to the hallway. They got to a door. Zack unlocked it, and they stepped in. Unlocking the door. Bridgette gasped.

The room was illuminated by neon lights, but that was not the spectacular thing about it. It was the content. The walls were lined with straps and cuffs. A wooden headboard fitted with chains and cuffs was perched in the center of the room. There was no bed. Dildos of all shapes and sizes were arranged in a corner, along with a bunch of ropes. Two long leather straps dangled from the ceiling. Two large wardrobes lined each side of the room.

"Wow. This is ..."

"Remarkable, right?" He held her face, looking into her eyes. "Are you sure you can handle it?"

"Yes."

"I'm sorry?" He raised an eyebrow.

Bridgette swallowed. "Yes ... master."

He grinned, before lowering his face. He brushed his lips across hers, withdrawing just as quickly. He walked to the center of the room, folding his hands across his chest.

"Take off your dress. Slowly." His tone was deep and commanding.

She slid the straps of the dress off her shoulders with care. She pulled the dress down, wiggling her hips. The silky material fell in a heap at her feet. All that was on her was her silver necklace and her lingerie, complete with a garter belt.

"Good. Come over here."

Bridgette complied, taking long, slow strides across the room.

"Now turn around."

As she did, he slapped her butt with such ferocity that she jumped.

Zack took out a blindfold from one of the wardrobes and tied it around her eyes. She didn't move an inch. When he was done, he slapped her butt again. She let out a low whimper.

"You've been a good girl so far. I'm impressed."

"Thank you, master."

He sucked air between his teeth. "Good girls don't speak unless they're told to. I'll have to correct that."

He fetched a mouth plug from one of the cabinets and placed it over her mouth. Bridgette squirmed. He held her waist, pressing his lower body against her. His cock pushed against her butt through his trousers as he leaned closer. She wriggled her ass, pushing back against him. He groaned.

"Not so fast."

Zack returned to the wardrobe and pulled out some wrist cuffs and chains. The rattle of the chains made Bridgette gasp with anticipation. He barked out another order as he attached the chains to the cuffs.

"Hold out your hands."

She stretched out her hands without delay. He attached the cuffs to her hand and chained them to the straps dangling from the ceiling. Heat crept up her body.

Zack slid his hands around the curve of her hips and up to her belly—her skin was incredibly soft. He grabbed her hips and pulled her hard against his cock once more. She whimpered, grinding against him.

"Are you that eager for me to fuck you?"

She nodded in reply.

"Not yet. Let's see how ready you are, first."

He bit her ear while his hands slid inside her panties to her eager cunt. She was warm to the touch and dripping wet. She wriggled against his fingers and he growled.

"Don't move," he ordered.

She stopped with a muffled moan. The look of agony on her face was his prize. She couldn't even beg to have him inside her. He had total control.

Gliding his finger across her clit, he separated her lips to find her drenched inside. As he dipped one finger into her warm wetness, her knees buckled underneath. His grip around her waist grew tighter. She whimpered even louder as he slid his finger back across her clit.

"You're soaking wet. You like being dominated, don't you?"

Zack brought his finger to his mouth to savor her sweetness as he held on to her, pressing his bulge against her ass. A low chuckle escaped his lips. Little beads of sweat rolled down her back and arms as she pulled on the chains. She couldn't go much longer without having him in her.

"It's time for your lingerie to disappear."

His hands went to the fastenings of her lingerie, exploring her body as he went. He undid her bra and garter belt, before slipping her stockings off her legs. She had nothing on now. He was still fully dressed.

"Get on your knees."

Zack flipped a switch on the wall that loosened the straps, allowing Bridgette to move more freely. She got on her knees. He removed the mouth gag, which was wet with her drool. He unzipped his trousers. Cupping her face in his hands, he took her lips in a heated kiss. He bit her lip. She stroked his tongue with hers, moaning into his mouth. He withdrew his lips from hers, planting little kisses on her temples.

"Please, master," she pleaded.

His lips teased her earlobes. "Tell me what you want."

"Please fuck me." She whimpered.

"How bad do you want my cock in you?"

"So bad. Give it to me, master. Make me yours!"

He smirked. "Good girl. Bend over."

Zack stroked her ass with the tip of his cock. Her begging and squirming continued, and so did his teasing. After moments of teasing, he held her waist.

"I'm going to fuck you now. Don't speak unless I tell you to."

She nodded in reply.

Zack tossed aside the rest of his clothing. He laid his arms around Bridgette, guiding himself into her. Her legs trembled as his cock slid with ease into her warm cunt. Taking in all of him, she moved her hips. He groped her tits with one hand and she threw her head back as the sensation overwhelmed her.

He straddled her ass as his cock drove into her until he was buried to the hilt. He covered her mouth with his hands, and she sucked a finger in. She arched her ass up toward him, giving him a perfect opportunity to plunge deeper into her. He moved his body against hers, fucking her with raw energy.

Bridgette trembled as Zack's cock dug deeper inside her slick cunt. He grabbed onto the headboard on either side to brace himself as he pounded into her harder. He thrust his cock into her wetness as hard and as deep as he could. Her body vibrated, shaken by an orgasmic tsunami that overwhelmed every part of her. Moans escaped her lips – she couldn't help herself.

She fell back into his arms and he held her tight while the aftershocks of her climax swept through her body. He kissed her neck.

"You did well. It's not over yet, though."

He fetched a bottle of lube and rubbed some on his still-erect cock.

"Now, I'm going to fuck your ass. Free yourself. Submit to my control. Remember, do not utter a word."

He pressed his lubed cock against her tight asshole. She'd had anal sex only once before, and it wasn't as intense as this. He guided himself in. She was tight, and he wouldn't have it any other way. He pushed into her hard and fast, and again, pounding her until her body shook once more. He lifted her thighs and plunged deeper into her. Her blindfold was wet with tears. Their bodies were slippery with sweat as they moved against each other.

"You're mine, right now, right here. All mine," Zack said in a hoarse voice.

Bridgette's body shook and shuddered once more as another wave of climax overtook her. Zack groaned as he dug deep into her one last time, flooding her insides with his cum. He kept his cock balls deep inside her for a minute until he was drained.

At that moment, the deep tide of passion turned to tenderness. Zack removed Bridgette's cuffs and her blindfold. Her face was flushed as she sunk into him. He lifted her off the ground, leading her out of his special room and into his bedroom. He laid her on the sheets and leaned over her. Their lips met.

"You did good," Zack said. "And now it's time to reward you."

His tongue moved over her body until he reached her pussy. Bridgette gasped as he lapped against her cunt.

Zack lifted his head. "You don't have to do anything. Just submit to me."

That was an order she didn't hesitate to follow.

Story 5: Good Little Maid

"**H**appy birthday, baby! I love you!"

"Thanks, love. I love you too. You told me you've got a surprise for me. The suspense is killing me! Can I know what it is now?"

Vera looked up at her boyfriend, Mark. She shook her head and giggled. It was true she promise him something, but did he have to bring it up now? At the moment, she was all cuddled up with him.

"I guess you're as impatient as ever, huh?"

He smiled. "I wouldn't be if I knew what it was."

Vera sprung to her feet. "Alright, baby. You'll get your surprise soon. Just, promise me you'll stay here. Okay?"

"I won't move an inch. Cross my heart."

"Great. I'll be right back."

She rushed to the bathroom, leaving Mark wondering what the surprise was. Ever since she told him a week ago she had a massive surprise for him on his birthday, he hadn't been able to get it off his mind. He tapped the floor with his right foot. It couldn't be dinner. Tickets to see a movie or show, maybe? He sighed. He would rather have dinner for two.

In the bathroom, Vera fetched a package she had kept for this moment. She opened the box, and a wide grin played on her face. Mark was in for a big one.

After what seemed like an eternity for Mark, the bathroom door opened. He heaved a sigh of relief.

"Finally. I thought you weren't–"

Mark stopped. His jaw dropped. Vera was dressed as a maid. Her ensemble was gorgeous: a very short dress with a ruffled cut at the top which exposed a lot of cleavage. She held a duster in one hand.

"I'm going to clean now, master. Is there any place that isn't tidy?" Her voice was tiny and breathy.

"Vera? What....what's going on?"

She feigned a gasp, holding one hand to her mouth. Wide-eyed, she pointed to a coffee table nearby.

"Goodness! This table is dusty. Looks like it's time for me to clean! Let's get this table shiny!"

She bent over to dust the table, offering Mark a tantalizing glimpse of her thighs and her ass. He licked his lips. So *this* was the surprise. Not bad.

Mark was a huge lover of cosplays and roleplays. It was a major turn-on for him whenever someone took on another role different from their nature. Vera was tough as nails. She'd always been the more dominant type – it was one of the reasons he found her attractive.

He'd mentioned to her once that it'll be his dream to see her as a submissive maid one day. She'd dismissed that fantasy. Who would've known she could take on that role?

"Ver–maid, that's enough. Get over here."

Vera hopped over to him. There was a false look of innocence in her eyes. Mark grinned. Time to test the waters.

He stood and went over to the table. Running a finger through the ebony surface, he shook his head.

"You've been a bad maid. There's still some dust here."

"Oh no! I'm so sorry, master! I would do anything to be a good maid again!"

He strutted over to her. "Anything?"

She nodded.

"In that case, you're going to suck my cock like the filthy little maid you are."

Mark cringed inwardly. He was sprouting clichéd dialogues now.

"Master ... will I become a good maid if I do that?"

He unzipped his pants. "Sure, you will. Now, get down."

Vera knelt on the carpet. Mark's cock sprang out, hitting her face. She wrapped her arms around it, fixing her gaze on him.

"Wow. It's lovely. Can I...put it in my mouth? Please?"

Her tone was soft. She appeared wide-eyed and innocent.

If there's one thing Vera wasn't, it was *innocent*.

"Yeah. Stick that cock in your mouth like a good maid."

Her tongue darted out to touch the tip. She stroked the crown of his cock, making him shudder. After some light teasing, she took half his length into her mouth in a go. He held her head with his hands, guiding her movement. His fingers gripped her hair at the roots, forcing her neck forward.

Her eyes were fixated on him as she bobbed up and down on his cock. He moved his hips, driving his cock deeper into the crevices of her mouth. His head rolled back as the tip of his cock nudged against her throat. His breaths were fast and heavy. He bit his lip and soon his cock began twitching. She took him as deep as she could before her gag reflex made her cough.

"That's a good girl," he said in a low voice.

He rammed his cock down her throat a couple of more times before pulling out. His cock glistened with her spit.

"Now turn around. I need to get a taste of that tight pussy."

Vera turned. Laying on the couch, she wriggled her butt to her master. Mark slapped her ass cheeks.

"Ready to serve your master?

"Yes sir! I'm ready!"

Grinning, he pulled her soaked panties down and tossed them aside. He pressed a finger to her clit, moving down to her dripping cunt.

Mark smirked. "Looks like someone likes being a good little maid."

His thumb slipped into her pussy, making her whimper. He brought another finger to tease her clit and her knees trembled, nearly giving way under her.

He withdrew, drawing nearer. He pushed the tip of his cock forward until it nestled against her cunt's opening, taunting her with its closeness. She drew in a sharp breath as his thick cock plunged into her. He held her hips, driving himself further. She gasped as his cock filled her insides to the brim. His hips moved, building up the pace with every thrust.

Mark grabbed Vera's hair. "Do you want me to fuck you good and hard, now that you've been such a good girl?"

"Yes... please yes..." Her voice came out as a gasp, desperate and pleading.

"Tell me. Tell me you want it."

"I want it. I want you. Please fuck me, Master!"

Vera rocked her hips against Mark, aiming to take him deeper. Her juices dribbled out around him, trickling down her thighs and coating his cock.

Vera squeezed her eyes shut as Mark's pace built. His hips slapped against the trembling flesh of her thighs. He tapped her ass as his movement increased. He gritted his teeth and held her waist, bringing all of his strength down onto her. Every stroke of his propelled her forward, sending tingles down her spine that preluded an electric climax.

"Oh fuck, master, you feel so good!"

Mark's fingernails raked over Vera's ass, and she shuddered without control as his thrusts came in hard. He pounded her faster, panting. His eyes rolled back and he plunged to new depths. He flicked a finger across her clit, making her body shudder again.

The minute sensation of his cock fucking her and his fingers playing with her clit sent her over the edge. Her body trembled as she came and she collapsed on the couch.

Mark wasn't done yet. His movements in and out of her cunt prolonged her orgasm. He pounded her harder. Faster. His cock throbbed and he groaned, burying himself deep in her. He released his semen inside her, grunting as the spurts of cum escaped his cock.

"Fuck. That was awesome." He sat on the far end of the couch.

Vera took a deep breath. "It was. We should do it again sometime."

"Why not now? I'm not done yet."

She gasped as she glanced at him. His cock was erect once more.

"Mark ... I mean, master, wasn't that enough?"

He grinned. "Not by a long shot. And it's Mark now. Playtime's over."

He held her by the hand and led her to the bedroom. She stripped out of her maid outfit and lay on the bed. She stretched her hand to him and he leaned over her.

"Ready for round two?"

Vera nodded. He lowered his lips to kiss her. His hands moved around her body. He gripped her thighs, guiding his cock inside her with his hips. She was still wet so it slid all in at a go. She wrapped her legs around his butt, pressing him closer to her.

Moaning, she dug into his shoulders with her manicured nails. He shoved his cock in, causing her to shiver. He didn't let up but thrust harder with every movement of his hips. She gasped and slammed her arms down onto the bed. Her back arched, as torrents of pleasure overtook her in rapid succession. Mark paused when he was inside her. He pulled out slowly, and she came again.

Mark pushed her legs by the back of her knees, keeping them in place with his hands as he aimed for her pleasure spot. He thrust his hips a few more times before she experienced yet another core-shaking climax. This time, she squirted hard in a gushing and arching stream. Her cunt clamped so tight on his cock that he shook as he released wads of cum into her.

Breathing hard, Mark collapsed next to Vera. She nestled up against me and brought her hand down to grip his flaccid cock. She stroked it a little, as more of a comforting gesture than an attempt to turn him on. He wraps his hands around her.

"Best birthday gift ever. Thanks, love."

Vera kissed him. "You deserve it, babe."

"When will we have our next roleplay session?" he asked after a moment of silence.

"As soon as we rest up, then take a shower. I'll be a naughty student, and you a strict teacher aching to spank me."

Mark laughed. "Can't wait."

Story 6:
Well-Serviced

♥

D^{*ing!*}

Ava stepped out of the elevator, into the brightly lit hall-way of the Chateau Del Rey, one of the top hotels in the Lyon area of France. Her eyes lit up, and her lips fell open as she took in the ambiance of the top-floor lobby. The golden chandelier among others was one of the things that made her want to stand in one spot, gawking like a little girl in Disneyland. Everything screamed top class and expensive. Even the guests of the hotel, walking about the lobby looked top class and expensive in their Italian suits, and dresses from a god-knows-what designer. Her chest tightened as she looked down at her black velvet mini-dress. The outfit was expensive, and she would have felt good about it if it wasn't a loan from her roommate.

Focus, Ava.

Inhaling deeply, she let out a loud sigh and tucked strands of her straight blonde hair, behind her ear. She walked over to the counter, head held high, and nodded to the receptionist.

"Bonsoir. Welcome to the Chateau Del Rey."

The receptionist smiled. Her pink lips were thin, and the cheekbones were high. Her pitch-black eyes glinted through her glasses, and her curly blonde hair was also done in a ponytail.

"How can I help you today?" she asked with a very thick French accent.

Ava turned down to her black leather purse. Her hand dove in, fingers fishing around till she pulled out a card. It contained the address of her client.

"I'm here to see Mr... Louis Gregorio... he's supposed to be in room 254."

The receptionist looked at her computer, clicking away.

"A wing, or B wing?" she asked without looking up.

"Wha–" Ava looked a the card again. "Oh... that's A wing. Sorry about that."

The receptionist gave a tight-lipped smile, still typing away on her computer. After a moment, she turned to pick up the telephone receiver beside her.

"Do you have an appointment?" she asked, placing the receiver between her ear and shoulder.

"Yes!... yes I do." She nodded quickly.

The receptionist dialed a number, then waited for the person at the other end to pick up.

"Bonsoir Monsieur. We have a lady here, she says she has an appoin–" she paused, listening to the person speak. Her gaze turned back to Ava, and she covered the receiver's mouthpiece with her palm.

"Name?"

"It's um... Ava. Ava Meyers."

She returned to the phone call, and after a minute, she dropped the receiver, turning back to Ava with a bright smile.

"Monsieur Gregorio is expecting you."

She gave her directions, and Ava walked away. A moment passed, and she finally got to room 254 A. She looked left and right across the hallway, then took in a deep breath before she stepped forward to knock. The door swung open, and a man peeked out. Her client, Mr. Gregorio. His lips curled up in a smirk, as he eyed her.

He stepped back, opening the door wider. Ava walked into the suite, and to her surprise, there were two other men seated there. They were well-dressed in white shirts and ties, with their suit jackets hanging on their arms.

Ava swallowed. Men in white shirts had always been her undoing.

"What a pleasant surprise." She turned to Louis with a smile. "I'm guessing your friends went to join the party?"

She turned back to the men. One of them was smoking a cigar, while the other had a drink in hand, staring at her with a glint in his eyes.

"I'll pay you three times your normal fee. Is that acceptable to you?"

Ava didn't have to think about it. Watching the men as they stared at her with desire burning in their eyes made her core clench with need.

This will be fun.

One of the men winked at her. Ava grinned and raised her gaze to meet Louis'.

"Alright. I accept your terms."

"Perfect." Louis clapped, turning to the guys. He pointed to the guy with the cigar. "That's Henshaw, the other guy is Cole."

The guys rose from their seats and started to pull off their shirts and ties. Ava dropped her bag on the nearest chair. She reached for her side, pulling down the zipper. She took off the dress and placed it on the same chair. All three guys were totally naked now.

"Come," Louis said, stepping forward. He pulled her closer, staring at her through piercing hazel eyes, before pressing his lips against hers. He tasted of vodka and lime. Ava moved her lips against his, but couldn't really get into the kiss. Her eyes were open, and she stared at the other guys, who were stroking their cocks, watching her. Soon enough, Henshaw, the tallest of the bunch came up to hold her from behind. He kissed her neck, circling his arms around her waist. Her eyes started to slide shut, as his lips on her neck sent a buzz down her body. Even the smell of the cigar on his lips intoxicated her. She angled her neck to give him more access, deepening the kiss with Louis. Henshaw's hands slid down her waist. His fingers trailed the outline of her panties, and his palm cupped one of her ass cheeks. Louis dropped his face to trail kisses down into her cleavage. One of his hands circled her back, and in one swift motion, he unhooked her bra. Ava pulled it off and dropped it on the floor.

Louis's sea-blue eyes turned darker as he stared at her D-cup boobs.

"Beautiful," he breathed, licking his lips. He cupped both boobs, then squeezed gently. Ava inhaled sharply as her nipples tightened in response. She dropped her hands, wrapping one around his hard cock, and stroking him from base to tip.

"Fuck... yes," Louis breathed, closing his eyes. He rubbed his fingers around her nipples and she jolted. Her body tingled, and a ball of sensation started to form in her center.

"Alright," Cole, who had been watching from afar, said. He picked up his drink and downed it in one quick gulp. "It's my turn."

He closed the distance between them and cupped one of Ava's boobs. He dropped his face and covered her nipple with his wet mouth.

"Oh god..." she moaned, burying her hand in his bushy brown hair. His tongue swirled over her nipple. His other hand slid down to trail the outline of her panties. He tucked his fingers into both sides of her panties and pulled them down. Ava quickly stepped out of it, using her foot to kick it to the side. Cole pulled back and stroked his cock. His hand slid up, and he held her by the hair, before guiding her face toward his dick. Henshaw held her by the waist, bending her over as she took Cole's cock in her mouth. He dropped to his knees before her, spreading her ass cheeks apart. His tongue dove in, lapping through her folds.

Ava's senses swam, as Henshaw's tongue sent a sharp wave of pleasure. Goosebumps rose on her skin as his tongue swirled around her clit. She tried to concentrate on Cole's cock in her mouth, but it was getting harder. Cole pulled back, slapping his cock on her cheek, before sliding it back in.

"Now suck that dick like you mean it," he said.

Ava nodded, closing her palm around his cock. She pumped his shaft furiously, while her tongue swirled around his tip.

"Oh god yes..." Cole nodded and closed his eyes. He grabbed a bunch of her hair, thrusting slowly into her mouth.

Henshaw rose from behind her, stroking his cock. In one fluid motion, he slid into her.

Ava moaned with Cole's cock in her mouth. Henshaw was big. One of the biggest cocks she had taken in some time. He stretched her to a maddeningly pleasurable level, and her eyes rolled back as he moved inside her. She pulled back from Cole's cock to let out a loud moan.

"Oh goddd!" she heaved.

The guys laughed.

"Henshaw's cock always has that effect on the ladies," Louis said, stroking his cock from a couch in the distance. Henshaw pulled back, and so did Cole.

"Come on," Henshaw guided her by the wrist towards the couch where Louis was seated. Louis chuckled lightly, as he pulled out a bottle of lube from the dresser beside the couch. He poured some on his hands and used it to lubricate his length.

"I'm more of an ass guy myself," he said.

Ava's eyes widened slightly as she stared at his cock. He wasn't as big as Henshaw's, but he was also above average. Louis reached out and held her by the waist. Turning her around, he made her sit on his lap. Next, he held on to his cock, and pushed against her asshole. It didn't go in on the first try, so he grabbed the lube again. He poured in a generous amount and tried again.

"Fuck..."

Ava bit down on her lip, as his cock slid into her asshole. He stilled for a moment, letting her get familiar with his size, then he started to move slowly. Henshaw moved closer, leaning in to slide his cock back into her wet sheath. Cole also stood by the side of the couch. He held on to her hair and guided his cock back into her mouth. The feeling was unlike anything she had ever felt before. She had never been filled in all three holes at the same time, and as odd as it was, the pleasure was incomparable. The guys moved in sync, pumping into her with a gradual increase in pace. Soon enough, the pleasure became too much to hold on to.

She moaned against Cole's twitching cock as her insides exploded in a cloud of pleasure. Her pussy clenched against Henshaw's cock, sending him off on his own orgasm. Her knees tensed, and her hips convulsed as the fireworks exploded.

"Fuck I'm gonna cum!" Cole grunted, pulling his cock swiftly out of her mouth. He stroked himself as quickly as he could, shooting warm streams of cum all over her lips and face. His legs tensed and toes curled as his orgasm hit in waves. Louis came last, spilling himself into her asshole. When it was over, they all sat on the chair, breathing heavily.

"Wow..." Louis breathed after a moment of silence. "That was a service well rendered."

Story 7: Practice Session

Brittany scrunched up her nose as she stared at her best friend Michelle's iPad screen. That was the first time she was seeing porn, and contrary to what was promised, she hated it.

"Alright." she rolled off the gray-colored queen-sized bed. "This is disgusting. I'm done."

"Wha–" Michelle looked up, turning her gaze to her best friend as she paced about the makeshift attic bedroom. "What do you mean? This is awesome." She turned back to the video, grinning wildly as she stared at the screen.

"No, it isn't." Brittany rolled her eyes. "Besides, it doesn't help me." She sighed, running her palms through her straight platinum-blonde hair.

"Of course it does." Michelle turned off the screen and placed the Ipad on her dresser beside the bed. She sat up, tucking her legs underneath.

"No it doesn't," Brittany snapped. "I don't even know the basics about sex, yet those guys are going at it like a bunch of rabbits." She gestured to the Ipad. Michelle stayed quiet, staring at her intently.

"What's going on with you?" she asked after a moment. Brittany stopped at the center of the room and turned to her. Heaving a soft sigh, she walked over to join her on the bed.

"I kissed Jason yesterday..." She bit her lips. "And it was bad."

"Wha–" Michelle stifled a giggle by clamping her palm over her lip.

"Go on." Brittany rolled her eyes. "Laugh all you want."

"I'm not–" Michelle shook her head, chuckling softly as she choked back another giggle. "I'm not laughing."

"Whatever," Brittany waved her off. "Forget I told you." She wanted to crawl off the bed, but Michelle held her wrist.

"Hey... come on now." She pulled her back. "Okay, I'm sorry. Tell me all about it."

Brittany stared at her for a minute before settling right across from her.

"We were at the park last night, watching the stars when he suddenly leaned in and kissed me." She paused to gauge the reaction on Michelle's face. The girl stayed blank, tucking back a strand of curly brown hair.

"I tried to stay cool and go with it," she continued, "but I ended up biting his lip."

"Damn." Michelle shook her head, scratching her shoulder over her thick wooly sweater. "You can't be that bad." she shrugged.

"Oh trust me. I am." Brittany nodded.

"No seriously," Michelle said. "Nobody is really bad at kissing. You just have to do it with someone who knows what they're doing."

"So…" Britanny drawled. "Are you saying Jason's the bad kisser?"

"Most likely, yeah." Michelle nodded.

"Damn." Brittany sighed. "What do I do now?"

After a moment of silence, Michelle shifted in her seat.

"I can help you practice… if you want." she shrugged.

"Y– you mean like…" Brittany trailed off.

"Yeah. it's no big deal really."

Brittany paused for a moment, fiddling with her fingers. "Are you sure it's okay? I mean… you're…"

"A lesbian?" Michelle huffed. "Please. You're my best friend. It won't be weird."

"Well… if you say so," she shrugged, shifting closer to her. Leaning in slowly, their lips touched, and Michelle cupped her face, moving her lips gently against hers. She angled her face, and slipped her tongue into Brittany's mouth, tasting the cranberry juice she had earlier. Brittany shuddered slightly, as the kiss spread jolts of pleasure through her entire body. She felt a tingle inside her like a flame that burnt stronger as the kiss intensified. Michelle was right. Jason had been doing it wrong.

"How's that?" Michelle asked as she pulled back. Her hazel eyes were dark, and her nostrils flared with each deep breath she took.

"It was…" Brittany gulped, "great." She forced a laugh. Staring down at her fingers, she licked her lips, tasting Michelle's strawberry bubblegum. Her insides continued to tingle, and when she couldn't take it anymore, she turned her gaze back to Michelle.

"Do you… wanna try again?"

"Ye—" Michelle cleared her throat. "Um… sure whatever… if you insist."

She leaned in again, Kissing her with even greater intensity. Brittany moaned into her mouth, sliding her palm up her sweater to cup her smooth olive face. Their lips fit together perfectly, and the tiny fire inside Brittany blossomed into a raging fire. She shifted even closer and pulled her lips away to trail kisses from Michelle's chin down to her neckline.

"And you said you weren't a good kisser," Michelle breathed, angling her neck to give her more access. Brittany chuckled.

"I'm learning from the best." Her palm moved down to cup Michelle's boob, kneading over the sweater.

"Fuck..." Michelle hissed, pulling the sweater over her head, and revealing her black cotton bra. She shifted even closer to Brittany, looking into her sapphire eyes as they darkened. Her gaze dropped to the pink colored blouse she had on and in one quick move, she pulled it over her head, dropping it on the ground. Brittany had on a pink colored sports bra, which she pulled off herself. Michelle inhaled sharply, staring hungrily at Brittany's heaving breasts. Her hands moved of their own volition and she wrapped them around each breast, kneading gently.

"Oh sh...it!" Brittany jolted. She pressed closer, arching her back as her nipples tightened, responding to Michelle's magic touch. Chuckling lightly, Michelle dropped her face, taking one boob in her mouth. She flicked her tongue around it till Brittany whimpered and muttered incoherently. Her wetness drenched her panties and seeped into her black leggings. Michelle turned to the other boob, giving it equal attention. Her palm slid from Brittany's boob down to her stomach, and lower.

"Ah... god Michelle..." Brittany groaned as Michelle used her fingers to rub her center over the thin fabric of her leggings. She held on to her wrist, rocking against her finger, as the pleasure dulled her senses. Michelle pulled back, tucking her hands into the sides of the leggings. She stared deep into Brittany's eyes, feeling the intensity of her lust, before pulling off her pants.

"Lie back," Michelle breathed, trailing her fingers along the outlines of Brittany's soaked panties. The girl promptly obeyed. She tucked a pillow behind her head and spread her legs wide. Michelle lay before her. Pulling her panties to the side, She leaned closer, taking in her intoxicating scent. She used a finger to brush through her tiny patch of hair, before covering her lips against her folds.

"Oh god!" Brittany gritted as Michelle lapped up her pussy juice. She used one hand to hold on to the pillow, while the other grabbed a bunch of Michelle's hair. She rocked slowly against her lips, shutting her eyes as she inched closer and closer to the edge. Michelle's tongue probed around her folds till she found her swollen clit. She sucked and swirled her tongue against it and Brittany writhed against her. Her insides clenched against Michelle's tongue as she was getting dangerously close to the edge. Michelle pulled back, to Brittany's disappointment.

"Wh– why did you stop?" she breathed.

"Oh come on," Michelle chuckled. "If you cum now, who's gonna take care of me?"

Brittany grinned widely, as she sat on the bed.

"My turn," she purred, leaning closer to kiss Michelle. Her hand slid up cup her boob, kneading briefly, before sliding lower. She unbuttoned Michelle's bum shorts, helping her pull them off, before using her fingers to cup her mound over the thin fabric of her lacy panties. Michelle sighed softly, biting her lips as her eyes slid shut. Brittany made slow circles around her mound, before pulling her panties aside. She slipped one finger into Michelle's wet sheath.

"Fuck yes!" Michelle groaned through gritted teeth. Her insides convulsed as Brittany started thrusting slowly into her. She rocked her hips against her fingers, and Brittany used her thumb to feel around till she found her clit. She tapped gently, flicking and swirling around till Michelle bit down on her lip to stifle a moan. The pleasure was spreading through her body like wildfire, and just when she thought it couldn't possibly get better, Brittany slipped in one more finger.

"God I'm... oh fuck..." Michelle muttered. She started to pick up her pace, but Brittany had other plans. She pulled back, tucked her fingers to her waist, and pulled off her panties. Michelle followed suit. Next, they swung their legs over each other, till their pussies were pressed against each other. They started to grind against each other, each moaning out the other's name as the pleasure rocked their entire being. Brittany came first. Her eyes rolled backward and her body jolted, sending her falling off the edge of the bed. Michelle's eyes slid shut, as her orgasm took over, spreading the buzz into every cell in her body. She gritted her teeth. Her muscles tensed, and her hips jerked intermittently, till her body couldn't move any longer. She slumped on the bed. They both stayed quiet for a moment, staring at the ceiling and breathing heavily. Brittany's eyes went wide as the clarity overshadowed by the moment of passion came to light.

"Oh shit," she muttered, gulping deeply. "What have we done?"

Story 8: Minerva's Punishment

Minerva stood in front of a tall brown door in a poorly lit hallway. She turned left and right before taking in a shuddered breath. Readjusting her black fur handbag, she took one step forward. She made to knock but stopped midway.

Damn it, Minerva. Why couldn't you just show some restraint?

She sighed softly, then knocked on the door. It opened almost immediately, and Toby stepped out. Toby, who she had come to know as 'master'. He had a blank look on his face as he stared at Minerva through piercing grey eyes. She couldn't meet his gaze. Her face stayed fixed on the ground and she bit her lip.

"Master," she muttered.

"We don't have a session today," he said. His voice was low, and it had a kind of rumbling tone to it.

"Yeah I know." she paused for a minute, taking another deep breath to help her nerves. "I did a bad thing."

"Speak," Toby said in a banal tone. It was as though he was incapable of raising his voice.

"I– I..." she sighed, turning to reach into her handbag. Her fingers fished around for a moment, till she pulled out a half-eaten cheeseburger, wrapped in a white patterned paper. Toby's gaze slid down to the burger in her hand. Without looking at her, he said.

"You ate a burger."

Minerva couldn't tell if it was supposed to be a question or a statement, but she chose the safer option.

"I– I'm sorry master," she rambled. "I didn't– it– I–"

"I told you not to eat junk food anymore."

"Yes you did master," she answered meekly, fiddling with her fingers. Toby watched her intently for a moment. The only hint of emotion visible on his face was the intermittent clenching of his jawline. After a long and tense silence, he stepped back and pulled the door open wider. Without a word, she stepped in.

The tiny living room was almost as dimly lit as the hallway. The fluorescent light flickered overhead, and the dim lamp on the table in front hardly illuminated anything.

"Drop your bag and come with me," Toby said and walked into the adjoining room, which was separated by a tall black door. Minerva pulled off the bag from over her head, and set it down on the brown couch, adjacent to the fireplace. Then she spun around and hurried to the door. Taking one last deep breath, she pushed it open and stepped in.

Toby's bedroom is not the regular type of room. Of course, there was a bed – a king-sized four-poster bed in the far corner of the room. But that wasn't the main focus of his room. Minerva turned her gaze to the other end of the room, where Toby had on display a range of whips, cuffs, and gags. Her heart pounded in her ears as Toby slowly walked past, trailing his fingers along the crimson wall while staring straight at her. A single drop of sweat rolled down the side of her head, falling off her chin. Her stomach twisted in knots as she waited with bated breath for what he was going to say and do to her. Thankfully, she didn't have to wait long.

"You disobeyed me, Minerva." He stopped right in front of her.

"I–" She took in another shuddering breath. "I'm sorry master, I–"

"Shh…" He placed his index finger against her lips, shutting her up. "Never interrupt me. That's the rule."

"Yes, master." She nodded. Toby angled his head, dropping his fingers to her chin. He raised her face to his level, staring at her big brown eyes.

"You did what I specifically told you not to do," he whispered, using his index finger to caress her chin. His touch sent a shiver through her. A mixture of anticipation and anxiety.

And lust.

Toby knew just how to stir those feelings in her. One look, one touch, one scolding, and she wanted to drop to her knees and ask him to punish her.

"You disobeyed me, Minerva."

She wanted to argue, wanted to tell him that she couldn't stop herself, but she bit her lip, forcing herself to keep silent.

"You know I have to punish you now."

Minerva inhaled sharply, as he walked back to the wall. He stared at the whip section for a while, before deciding on a black leather multiple-tailed whip.

"Take off your clothes," he commanded, fiddling with the whip's end.

Minerva promptly obeyed. She peeled off the buttons of her wine-colored shirt and took it off. Next, she tucked her fingers inside her black pencil skirt, pulling it down. She stepped out of it and stood before Toby in her black lacy one-piece lingerie. Toby's lips curled up in a smirk, as he eyed the underwear.

"Your lingerie is really sexy. That's good."

"Thank you, master." Minerva bowed slightly.

"Not sexy enough to not punish you." He shook his head. "But just enough to make me want to reduce the whipping."

He turned back to the wall, and picked out a silver handcuff. He walked over to an overhead steel bar, at the center of the room, and turned to Minerva. She came closer, stretching out both her hands, and they were cuffed over the bar. Toby walked over to a lever beside the bed. He pulled it, and the bar overhead shifted upwards, moving Minerva along with it. Toby walked up behind her, while she struggled to stand on the tip of her toes. Without worrying, he lashed her butt with the whip. Minera froze, as the stinging pain seared into her skin. She gritted her teeth, shaking like a leaf in the cold. But even with the overwhelming pain, she anticipated and welcomed the next lash.

Toby struck her backside for the second time. She jolted again, arching her back as she struggled to stay on her toes. The pain brought with it a burst of adrenaline that left her wanting more. Toby struck her one last time. His lips curled up into a smile as she whimpered helplessly. He dropped the whip, and he placed his palm on the warm skin where he had flogged her. She hissed slightly, but he didn't stop. He pressed himself against her back, still rubbing her pinkish skin.

"Damn. You look so fuckable right now," he whispered hoarsely into her ear. Without another word, he walked back to the lever and pulled it, letting her down. He led her by the cuffs to the edge of the bed and pushed her down till she fell to her knees. He quickly unbuckled his belt and dropped his pants. Then he reached into his boxers and pulled out his thick cock.

"Suck it," he commanded, slapping her lips with the tip till she opened her mouth.

She couldn't do much with her hands, because they were tied up, but her head bobbed up and down his cock. He grabbed hold of her long auburn hair, and pressed himself into her mouth, till he felt himself at the back of her throat. She gagged a bit and pulled back. The thick drool at the corner of her lips fell to the ground as Toby pulled her up and turned her around till she was facing the bed. Next, he pushed her till her body was perfectly arched, bent to do his bidding. He trailed his fingers along the outlines of her already-drenched lacy lingerie, and he hissed softly.

"Your lingerie has done its job."

Before Minerva could turn around to figure out what he meant, she heard the ripping sound of the ass area of the underwear. Spreading the fabric wide, he trailed his cock along the divide of her ass and pussy, positioning himself against her.

"I'm going to fuck you now," he said, pushing himself into her warm sheath.

"Fuck..." Minerva hissed as Toby's cock filled and stretched her. She wanted to touch him. She wanted to run her palms up his plaid jacket, and even bury them in his graying hair. But with the cuffs, she was at his mercy. Toby started to thrust into her, slowly at first, but when she started to meet his thrusts, he worked up a rhythm. Minerva bit her lips, as a low moan escaped her throat. The pleasure mixed with the stinging sensation of earlier floggings was sending her closer and closer to the edge. Toby slapped her ass, watching it jiggle against his cock. He started to pump faster as he drew closer to climax.

Minerva was close too, and he could tell by the way her pussy wrapped and clenched around his cock. He pulled out abruptly and yanked her hair backward. Turning her around and sinking her to her knees, he pried her mouth open, and slipped his cock in. She swirled her tongue around his tip, as he pumped, and he couldn't even complete four thrusts before his orgasm threw him off the edge.

"Fuck!" he said, pulling out his cock from her mouth. His muscles twitched and tensed as she shot his warm stream of cum on her face and chest. His knees jerked violently, and his toes curled as the pleasure swept through him in waves. When it was over, he picked up his pants and walked away. An unsatisfied Minerva started to slide her hands down to her pussy, hoping to complete her orgasm, but Toby stopped her.

"Don't touch yourself."

Minerva bit back a cry. A wicked smile crept up Toby's face.

"That's your punishment."

Story 9: Purple Lingerie

♥

Ding!

Brielle dropped the novel she was reading and turned her gaze to her phone. Grabbing it from the dresser beside her bed, she stared at the screen. It was a text from Damien, her sexting buddy. She clicked open the message.

"Oh, shit..." She sat up suddenly, reading and re-reading the text.

"I'm outside your apartment," she read out loud and dropped the phone. Her heart rate spiked, and her eyes darted around the white and purple-themed bedroom, looking for nothing in particular. She picked up the phone and read the text one more time, trying to tell whether it was a joke or not.

"That's not– that's not possible," she muttered under her breath. Damien was supposed to be in Madagascar, studying monkeys. How could he be in New York?

While they were texting the day before, he made some jokes about flying over to come to see her, but she hadn't taken him seriously. Even when he asked for her house address and apartment number, she only sent them to humor him. She didn't really think that he was being serious.

Ding!

She clicked on the new message he had sent. It was a photo. Her eyes went wide as she stared at the picture of Damien standing outside her apartment.

"He– he really is here!"

She sprang up from the bed, grinning wildly as she stopped in front of her full-length mirror to take a look at her outfit. She was wearing a white and green floral patterned cotton blouse, and a pair of faded blue skinny jeans.

Her phone dinged again, and she turned to it.

"Just give me one moment," she said, turning back to the mirror. Her straight blonde hair was done in a ponytail, and after a very intense internal battle, she decided to pull off the band and let her hair fall freely to her sides. She readjusted the blouse till it exposed a little more cleavage before turning around to walk out of the room. Reaching the door, she took in a deep breath, before opening it.

"Hi," Damien said in his deep baritone voice. His lips curled up as he looked at her from up to down through sea-blue eyes. Brielle took in a sharp breath as the intensity of his stare was starting to send tingles all around her body.

"H–hi," she managed. "Come on in."

He tucked both his hands into the pockets of his gray hoodie, then stepped in.

"Wow," he said, looking around at the numerous still-life paintings she had displayed in the tiny living room. His gaze rested on a nude female sculpture, sitting on the bookshelf above the fireplace. He reached out to touch it.

"So... what are you doing here?" she asked, closing the door behind her. I thought you were in Madagascar?"

"Isn't it obvious?" He turned around. "I'm here for you."

He closed the distance between them and wrapped his arms around her waist. Brielle gasped slightly as he pulled her closer, inhaling his rosewood and lavender scent.

"I couldn't get over the photo you sent me three days ago," he whispered into her ear. "That purple Lingerie did things to me. I just had to take the next flight in." He licked his lips while staring intently at hers.

"Please tell me it's still in your closet?"

"It's in the laundry," Brielle breathed. "But I assure you," she stood on her tippy toes till her lips were mere centimeters against his ear. "I'm wearing something way sexier..."

Damien's eyes grew dark with lust. He shuddered lightly as Brielle ran her lips against his ear lobe. He pulled her face closer, and pressed his lips against hers in a warm passionate kiss. His lips tasted like chocolate and sweet wine. She moaned into his mouth and angled her face as their tongues melded against each other.

"Fuck Brie..." Damien said, pulling back to draw a breath. "You taste so good."

He kissed her chin, then trailed kissed down her neckline till she shuddered.

"Take this off."

Brielle tugged at his hoodie till he pulled it off and flung it to one of the purple couches at the side. He was wearing a black body hug tee shirt underneath.

"Oh fuck," she breathed. She pressed against him, running her palms around the ridges of his toned abs.

"Your turn," Damien said in a throaty whisper. Her lips curled up in a mischievous smile, as she stepped back and pulled the blouse over her head.

"My god..."

When she said she was wearing something sexier, she wasn't lying. Her black lacy bra was an eye tease. It showed off way more than it covered. The fabric itself was almost see-through, and the only part of her full C-cup boob which was fully covered were her nipples. Damien's cock twitched painfully inside his levi pants as he continued to stare at his little slice of heaven. He gulped loudly when she took slow steps back to him. Wrapping her arms around his body, she kissed his chest over his shirt. Damien's hand crawled up to take one breast in hand, kneading gently.

"Oh Damien," she sighed as the tingles on her skin converged between her legs, drenching her panties. He dropped his other hand from her waist, lower till he had her ass cheek in hand. His fingers flicked her nipples over the soft fabric, and she jerked against him. She raised his shirt up, and he pulled it over his head, dropping it on the ground. He reached behind her, and with one flick of his fingers, her bra came undone. She pulled it off, then took both his hands, placing them on each of her breasts. He looked into her hazel eyes, before dropping his face to take one nipple in his mouth.

"Fuck!" Brielle moaned loudly as the pleasure shot through her. It spread into every cell in her body. She buried her hands inside his wavy brown hair, pushing him closer to her. Damien flicked and swirled his tongue around her nipple till they tightened in response. He did the same for the other, and soon enough, he had her squirming against him. Brielle guided him gently backward and pushed him till he sat on the chair behind him. She dropped to her knees and undid his belt buckle. Damien raised his hip and pushed off the jeans till they got to his knees. She reached into his boxers and pulled out his thick cock. Her eyes went wide, and her mouth fell slightly open.

"Fuck – you're huge!"

Damien let out a throaty laughter, readjusting himself on the couch as she stroked him from base to tip. His cock had thick veins stretching down to the base and the pink bulbous head was glazed with precum. Locking eyes with him, Brielle slipped his cock into her mouth, tasting his salty sweetness.

"Ahh yes..."

He sat back against the couch, eyes sliding shut as the pleasure dulled his senses. Her head bobbed up and down against his cock, slurping loudly. She pulled back and gathered the drool at the corner of her mouth, using it to lubricate and pump his shaft as quickly as she could. His cock started to twitch violently, and he held her wrist.

"No," he shook his head. "I can't finish yet."

She nodded, giggling with a glint in her eyes. Damien rose from his seat, and she stepped back. She tucked both thumbs into either side of her jeans, pulling them down. She stepped out of them, then took off her lacy panties. Finally, she stood before Damien, gloriously naked.

He shook his head, ravishing her with his eyes. "You are gorgeous."

She closed the distance between them with a sultry smile on her lips.

"I know," she whispered. "Now will you keep standing there? Or are you gonna fuck me?"

Damien needed no further invitation. He stepped out of his jeans and grabbed her by the waist. In one swift motion, he turned her around and bent her over till she was holding the edge of the couch.

"Oh and, just so you know..." he stood behind her, hands on both her ass cheeks. "I won't be fucking your pussy today. I'm more of an ass guy myself."

"What?" she breathed. "I– I don't—"

"Don't worry, Brie." He gathered her wetness in his fingers and rubbed it against her ass. "You're gonna love it. I promise. I came prepared."

He grabbed his pants off the floor and brought out a lube. Brielle sighed as he rubbed some of it on her ass. With that, he spread her ass cheeks apart and pushed himself into her.

"Oh my... god!" Brielle groaned, clutching tightly to the edge of the couch. There was a dull pain at first, but it soon got replaced with a feeling of euphoric pleasure. She couldn't believe that she had taken his monster cock in her ass. The feeling was so intoxicating that she spread her legs, ready to take as much as he could give. Damien didn't move for a moment. He let her get accustomed to his size, before starting with slow thrusts. Soon enough she got the rhythm and returned with thrusts of her own.

"Oh fuck, yes, Brie!" Damien hissed as he quickened the pace of his thrusts. Every time her ass clenched and unclenched was sending him closer and closer to the brink. Soon enough he couldn't hold on any longer, so he circled his arms around her. Rubbing furiously against her pussy lips, his fingers found her clit. He flicked once, then twice and–

Brielle cried out as her orgasm caught her by surprise. It swept through her like electricity, buzzing through every cell in her body. Her knees buckled, and her muscles tensed. Damien's orgasm followed. His hips jerked against her, as he spilled his cum into her ass. They both fell heavily against the chair, panting. Neither of them spoke for a while as they struggled to catch their breath.

"Wow..." Damien gulped. "That was intense."

"Better than phone sex," Brielle said between pants. "I hope you're not going back anytime soon."

Damien smiled and grabbed her, drawing her in for a kiss.

"I think I'll stay back for a couple days," he said against her lips.

Brielle smiled. "Perfect."

Story 10: Game Night

❤

"Is she here?"

Fred held out a finger to Monique, his girlfriend, as he peeked out the blinders of his bedroom window. He saw Cara, Monique's best friend, as she stepped out of her BMW convertible and raced across the lawn to the porch. He dropped the blinders and turned to her, a mischievous smirk curling up his lips.

"Yes she is."

"Okay good," Monique said, taking a deep breath. "We're just gonna stick to the plan right?"

"Hey..." Fred walked over to her, circling his big arms around her waist. "It's going to be alright."

"Do you think she'll be down?" Monique asked. Her hazel eyes were wide as she stared at him.

"I don't know." He shrugged. "Maybe. But we wouldn't know if we didn't ask."

"Shit." Monique shook her head, burying her face in her palm. "What if she finds it weird and says no? I don't want to lose my best friend."

"What if she doesn't?" Fred placed his palm on her chin, his thumb stroking her olive skin. "Either way–"

The door swung open, and Cara walked in with a plastic bag filled with junk food.

"We'll find out tonight," Fred said with a note of finality.

Cara glanced between them. "Okay! Good to know that I'm not the only one who's excited about tonight." Her emerald eyes glinted brightly. "I've got the snacks. Let the game night begin."

"Actually," Fred started. "We were hoping to play a different game tonight."

"Really?" Cara's smile faltered. "That's disappointing. I was hoping to play some charades." She sighed and turned to Monique. "So what game are we playing then?"

"How about a threeway?" Monique blurted out.

"What?" Cara asked, her thick brows furrowing as she looked from Fred to Monique. "What are you talking about?"

"Come on, Cara," Fred said. "I know you've thought about this. I know you've thought about it a lot." He paused for a moment as his lips curled up into a smile. "I've seen the way you look at me." He turned to Monique. "And I've seen the way you look at her."

"I know you want me... Cara," Monique took one bold step forward. "And I want you too. So why not just go for it? Give each other what we want?"

"Um." Cara's eyes were wide. "What if it's not–"

"Shh..." Monique placed her finger on Cara's lips. "It's okay. You don't need to say anything. If this is what you want, kiss me. And if not..."

Cara drew in a ragged breath as her gaze dropped to Monique's cherry lips. Cara licked her lips, eyes darkening. She reached out to touch Monique's arm. Monique inhaled sharply. Pulling her closer, Cara pressed her lips against hers, taking her mouth in a warm, passionate kiss. Her arms moved of their own volition. She dropped the plastic bag and ran her hands around Monique's back. Moaning softly, she angled her head and parted her lips as Monique's tongue slipped in. The strawberry taste in Cara's mouth made Monique smile, and she deepened the kiss. She trailed her tongue the outline of Cara's lips, with her hands sliding up to close around her neck.

"Fuck..." Fred moaned softly as the sight made the blood rush down his cock. He stroked the bulge in his pants while watching them. Monique pulled back from the kiss and turned to him.

"Are you waiting for an invitation or something?"

His Adam's apple bobbed up and down as he gulped loudly. He pulled off his plaid shirt and the plain black top he wore underneath. The girls looked at his ripped chest and the ridges of his toned abs. Turning back to themselves, they smiled knowingly, then walked over to him. Cara pulled him in for a kiss while Monique sank to her knees before him. She unbuckled his belt and pulled down his cargo pants before reaching into his boxers to pull out his thick cock. Grinning wildly, she inhaled the musky scent of his cock, then lapped up his salty precum before taking him in her mouth.

Fred moaned loudly into Cara's mouth. He pulled back and trailed kisses down her neck. His hands found the hem of her pink dress, and he pulled it over her head. Dropping the top on the bed, his eyes feasted on her heaving breasts. His fingers trailed the outlines of her black cotton bra. He turned his gaze to Monique, who was bobbing her head around his firm shaft. He used his free hand to grab a bunch of her straight black hair as he thrust it into her mouth. She gagged slightly, then pulled back to swirl her tongue around his pink tip.

"Fuck..." Fred groaned. He pulled his boxers all the way down and stepped out of them before turning back to Cara. He circled his arms around her and unhooked her bra. She pulled it off and dropped it on the ground. Monique followed suit, pulling off her blouse, then her bra. She rose from her knees and unzipped her black ripped jeans. Pulling it down, she stepped out of it, then turned to take both Cara's boobs in her hands. Kneading gently, she flicked her fingers over her nipples.

"Oh god..." Cara shuddered, biting her lips as her eyes fluttered shut. She reached a hand out to the back of Monique's neck, sliding up to her head. She pulled her closer, guiding her to her boob. Monique smiled as she covered her nipple with her wet mouth. Cara shuddered as the pleasure sent sparks through her body. Moisture pooled between her legs and soaked her panties. Monique used her tongue to flick and tease her nipples until Cara started muttering incoherently. She pulled back, chuckling. Fred took over. He guided Cara back to the bed, laying her gently. He quickly pulled off her grey jeans and then her black panties. Sinking to his knees before her, he kissed her toes, sucking one after the other, before moving forward to trail kisses up her slender legs. His palm cupped her thigh, and he caressed them as his lips inched closer and closer to her pussy.

"Oh god!" Cara groaned as Fred's lips closed over her slick cunt. His tongue swirled around her folds as he lapped up her juices. Cara slid her hand up his curly brown hair, pressing him against her as she ground against his face. His tongue found her swollen clit, and she writhed and thrashed against him. Next, he pulled back and rose to his feet. He grabbed her waist, pulled her to the edge of the bed, and then locked her thighs around his waist. Monique held his cock, stroking gently from base to tip, before guiding him into Cara's wet velvety center.

"Gaa... fuck!" Cara moaned as Fred's thick shaft slid into her, filling her. He readjusted her thighs around his waist before thrusting slowly. Monique crawled up the bed to lay by Cara's side. She silenced her moans by taking her lips against hers. She took Cara's hand and guided it to her already-soaked panties. She moaned slightly as Cara pulled her panties aside and slipped one finger into her. Monique rocked her hips against Cara's finger thrusts. Her eyes closed, and she held on to her wrists, rocking faster.

Watching the girls was enough to send Fred close to climax. The feel of Cara's tight pussy around his cock sent him even closer. His thrusts became faster and more erratic as he gritted his teeth, holding on for dear life. Monique was also close. She pushed off Cara's hands, took off her panties, and threw them on the floor. She rolled on top of Cara, then positioned herself against her mouth. Cara's eyes slid shut as she drank in Monique's pussy juice. Her tongue lapped against her folds, flicking and probing till she found her clit.

"Oh god!"

Monique moaned as Cara's tongue made circles around her swollen clit. She held onto the wooden bedpost as she rocked against her lips.

The pleasure pushed her to the edge of the precipice, and with one last flick of Cara's tongue, she was done. Her whole body tensed and shivered as the pleasure exploded in her.

"Fuckkk..."

She gritted her teeth as her tremors wracked her body. When it was over, she rolled off and slid her palm down to Cara's center. Her fingers found her clit, and she stroked it gently. That did it for Cara.

"God I'm–"

Her pussy clenched around Fred's cock as pleasure swept through her.

Fred's orgasm caught him by surprise as Cara's clenching pussy flung him over the edge. His fingers dug into her thigh, hips jerking intermittently as he shot warm streams of cum into her. He collapsed onto her stomach when he was spent, and they both stayed still as they caught their breath. A few minutes passed, and Cara turned to stare at the ceiling.

"Oh shit." She turned to Monique, who was still breathing heavily. "Did I just fuck your boyfriend?"

Final Words

♥

Hi there, this is Mia Foster, and I hope my naughty short sex stories have left you craving for more. But to make sure that I'm delivering exactly what you desire, I need your help.

I'd love to know what stories got your heart racing and your pulse pounding. By leaving an honest review on the product page, which will take less than 60 seconds of your time, you'll help me create more tantalizing tales.

Not only that, but you'll also be giving other readers the chance to discover these steamy and seductive short stories! So, what are you waiting for? Let's make these stories even hotter together!

Yours truly,

Mia Foster.